TIMELESS CLASSICS

AROUND THE WORLD IN EIGHTY DAYS

Jules Verne

– ADAPTED BY –

Janice Greene

SADDLEBACK
EDUCATIONAL PUBLISHING

TIMELESS CLASSICS

Literature Set 1 (1719-1844)

A Christmas Carol
The Count of Monte Cristo
Frankenstein
Gulliver's Travels
The Hunchback of Notre Dame
The Last of the Mohicans

Oliver Twist
Pride and Prejudice
Robinson Crusoe
The Swiss Family Robinson
The Three Musketeers

Literature Set 2 (1845-1884)

The Adventures of Huckleberry Finn
The Adventures of Tom Sawyer
Around the World in 80 Days
Great Expectations
Jane Eyre
The Man in the Iron Mask

Moby Dick
The Prince and the Pauper
The Scarlet Letter
A Tale of Two Cities
20,000 Leagues Under the Sea

Literature Set 3 (1886-1908)

The Call of the Wild
Captains Courageous
Dracula
Dr. Jekyll and Mr. Hyde
The Hound of the Baskervilles
The Jungle Book

Kidnapped
The Red Badge of Courage
The Time Machine
Treasure Island
The War of the Worlds
White Fang

SADDLEBACK
EDUCATIONAL PUBLISHING
www.sdlback.com

Copyright ©2001, 2011 by Saddleback Educational Publishing

ISBN-13: 978-1-61651-070-1
ISBN-10: 1-61651-070-6
eBook: 978-1-60291-804-7

Printed in the U.S.A.

20 19 18 17 16   3 4 5 6 7

| Contents |

| 1 |

A Daring Bet

In 1872, Mr. Phileas Fogg lived in a fashionable part of London. People there knew almost nothing about him.

Was Phileas Fogg rich? Certainly, he was rich. And he was often generous. But how had he made his money? No one would think of asking him such a question.

He spoke very little. This made him seem even more mysterious. His daily habits could easily be observed. But everything he did was precisely what he had always done.

Had he traveled? Most likely he had. No one seemed to know the world better.

He seemed to have neither wife nor children. He lived alone—a single servant was all he needed. But Phileas Fogg was not an easy master. On the first of October, he fired his servant, James

Forster. Forster had brought him shaving water that was 84 degrees instead of 86!

On October 2, Mr. Fogg waited for his new servant to arrive. He watched his clock. It showed the hours, the minutes, the seconds, the days, the months, and the years.

Then Fogg heard someone knocking. When he answered the door, a young man of about 30 stepped forward and bowed.

"You are a Frenchman, I believe," said Phileas Fogg, "and your name is John?"

"*Jean*, if you please, monsieur," the man said. "Jean Passepartout. You probably know that *passepartout* means 'go everywhere' in French. I have this name because I have gone from one business to another. I've been a singer and a circus-rider. I've been a professor of gymnastics and a fireman. But I left France to become a valet in England. I heard that you are the most exact and regular gentleman in the country. I have come to you with the hope of living a quiet life. I now wish to forget the name Passepartout."

"Passepartout suits me," Mr. Fogg said. "I have heard many good things about you. It is now exactly twenty-nine minutes past eleven A.M. Today is Wednesday, October second, and you are now in my service."

With that, Phileas Fogg put on his hat and went out the door. He said not a word. Passepartout was alone in the house.

During his brief talk with Mr. Fogg, Passepartout had studied him carefully. Mr. Fogg seemed to be about 40 years old. He was a tall, well-built man. His features were fine and handsome. His hair and whiskers were light. His eyes were calm and clear.

Fogg never made a move that was not necessary. He never took an extra step. Wherever he went, he went by the shortest route. He avoided most people's company, knowing they would slow him down.

Passepartout had searched in vain for a master after his own heart. He was an honest man, with a pleasant face. He had a good, round head. It was the kind of head one likes to see on the shoulders of a friend. His body was compact, solid, and muscular.

Now Passepartout explored Mr. Fogg's house from top to bottom. It was warm and quiet and very clean—like a snail's shell.

Above the clock, Passepartout found a list of his duties. Tea and toast were to be served at

23 minutes past eight. Shaving water was to be brought at 37 minutes past nine. The duties went on and on until midnight, when Mr. Fogg went to bed.

Mr. Fogg's clothes were many, and in the best taste. Each pair of pants, each coat and vest had a number. The numbers showed the time of year they were to be worn. The same system was used for his shoes.

Passepartout rubbed his hands. A wide smile spread across his face.

This is exactly what I wanted! he said to himself. *We shall get along very well, Mr. Fogg and I! What a regular gentleman he must be— a real machine!*

After leaving the house, Phileas Fogg walked to the Reform Club. He took his place at his usual table and ate his breakfast. At 13 minutes to one, he read a newspaper. At a quarter to four he read another paper until dinner time. After dinner, five other members of the Reform Club arrived. They usually played a game of whist with Mr. Fogg.

Flanagan was a brewer. Stuart was an engineer. Sullivan and Fallentin were bankers. And Ralph was a director of the Bank of England.

"Well," said Flanagan to the other men, "what

do you think about the big robbery?"

"It's a shame," Stuart said. "I daresay the money will never be found."

"On the contrary," Ralph said. "I think the robber *will* be found. Detectives have been sent to ports all around the world. The robber will have to be very clever to slip through."

All of London was gossiping about the robbery. Three days earlier, 55,000 pounds had been stolen from the Bank of England! The papers had described the thief as a well-dressed gentleman.

"The chances are in favor of the thief," Stuart said. "After all, he could hide anywhere. The world is big enough."

"It was once," Phileas Fogg said, in a low tone. Then he handed the cards to Flanagan, saying, "Cut, sir."

"Huh? What do you mean by *once*?" asked Stuart. "Has the world grown smaller?"

"It has!" Ralph said. "A man can now go around the world a hundred times faster than he could a hundred years ago."

"A man can now go around the world in eighty days," Phileas Fogg announced. "I have a newspaper article that says exactly that."

"*Perhaps* in eighty days!" Stuart objected. "But that doesn't account for bad weather, shipwrecks, railway accidents, and so on."

"All those things *are* taken into account," Mr. Fogg said, throwing down two trumps.

Stuart was excited. "So you say, Fogg. I'll bet you four thousand pounds that such a trip is impossible."

"On the contrary, it's quite possible," Mr. Fogg insisted.

"Well, make the bet then!" Stuart cried.

"Nothing would please me more," Phileas Fogg said. "I must warn you, though, that I am confident of my success. But if I should lose, I shall pay you twenty thousand pounds."

"Twenty thousand pounds!" Sullivan cried out in astonishment. "Why, you'd lose it all if a single accident made you late!"

"The unforeseen does not exist," Phileas Fogg said quietly. "I bet twenty thousand pounds that I can make a tour of the world in eighty days. Each of you bet four thousand pounds that I will fail. Do all of you accept?"

"We accept," said the five men.

"Very well," Fogg said. "The train leaves for Dover at a quarter to nine. I will take it."

"This very evening?" Stuart gasped.

"This very evening," Fogg assured him. "This is the second day of October. In eighty days, I shall be back here in this very room at the Reform Club. Let me see: That shall be the twenty-first of December, at a quarter to nine P.M. If I fail, my twenty thousand pounds will belong to you, gentlemen."

The bet was signed by every man. The 20,000 pounds was half of Fogg's fortune. The other half he would need for his journey.

The clock struck seven. The gentlemen offered to stop the game so that Mr. Fogg could get ready for his trip.

"I'm quite ready now," Fogg said calmly. "Let us continue the game, gentlemen."

| 2 |

En Route to Egypt

When the game was over, Mr. Fogg had won more than 20 pounds. At precisely 25 minutes after seven, he left the Reform Club.

Passepartout had expected his master to return at midnight. Imagine his surprise!

"We leave for Dover in ten minutes," Mr. Fogg announced.

Passepartout was puzzled. "Monsieur is going to leave home?" he asked.

"Indeed," Phileas Fogg said. "You and I are going around the world in eighty days!"

Passepartout was stunned. "But the trunks . . ." he sputtered.

"We'll pack no trunks, only a small bag," Mr. Fogg said. "Don't fret! We'll buy extra clothes along the way. Make haste!"

Passepartout dashed to his room. "All I wanted

was to live a quiet life!" he muttered.

By 8:00 P.M., Passepartout had packed a small bag with a few clothes.

At the door, his master handed him another bag. "Take good care of it," he said. "There are twenty thousand pounds inside."

Passepartout and his master took a cab to the railway station. There, a poor beggar-woman reached out to them. She had muddy, naked feet. In her arms, she carried a child.

Mr. Fogg gave her the money he'd just won at whist. Passepartout's eyes grew moist. His master's kindness had touched his heart.

Fogg bought two first-class tickets for Paris. As the train hurtled down the track, Passepartout gave out a cry of despair.

"What's the matter?" Mr. Fogg asked.

"Alas!" Passepartout cried. "In my hurry, I forgot to turn off the gaslight in my room!"

"So be it," Mr. Fogg said coolly. "Let it burn. But you must pay for it."

Word of Mr. Fogg's trip quickly spread around London. Only a few people sided with Mr. Fogg. Most shook their heads, saying his claim was ridiculous! Most of the London newspapers came out against him.

Soon people all over England were placing bets on whether or not Mr. Fogg would succeed. Phileas Fogg "bonds" were sold on the London exchange. For several days, they were very popular. One old gentleman, Lord Albermarle, proudly bet 5,000 pounds that Mr. Fogg would succeed.

"If the trip can be made at all," he said, "it ought to be made by an Englishman."

Then, one week after Mr. Fogg had left England, there was shocking news. Phileas Fogg was wanted for questioning by the London police! They suspected him of robbing the Bank of England.

The description of the bank robber was exactly like the portrait of Mr. Fogg. People reconsidered his mysterious ways and his speedy departure. To many, it now seemed clear that his trip around the world was actually a plan of escape.

* * * *

A ship called *Mongolia* was about to reach port at Suez, Egypt. Two men were waiting on the dock. One was the British consul at Suez. Another was a small, impatient man with eyebrows that twitched nervously. He was Mr. Fix, an English detective.

For the 20th time, the detective asked the consul, "Are you sure that the *Mongolia* is never late?"

"Have patience, Mr. Fix," the consul said. "She won't be late. But even if the suspect is on board, how will you recognize him?"

"Oh, I have a scent—like a sixth sense—for these fellows," Mr. Fix boasted. "It's part hearing, part seeing, and part smelling. I've arrested more than one of these gentlemen in my time. If Fogg is on board, he'll not slip through my fingers."

"But, sir!" the consul objected. "From your

description, it would seem that Fogg looks like any other honest man."

"Great robbers always look like honest folk," Mr. Fix said with a wink. "If you have the face of a rascal, there's only one thing you can do: live an honest life. Otherwise, you'll most surely be arrested soon enough."

Then several sharp whistles were heard and the great ship steamed into the port. After the anchor was dropped, some passengers stayed on deck. Most took small boats to shore.

Passepartout approached Mr. Fix as the passengers crowded the wharf. He was holding a passport and looking for the consul.

"I need to have a visa stamp put on this," he told Mr. Fix. "Who can do this for me?"

Studying the passport, Mr. Fix nearly jumped in surprise. It belonged to Mr. Fogg!

"Is this yours?" he asked.

"No, sir, it's my master's," Passepartout replied. "He's still on board the ship."

"Aha! Then tell him he must go to the consul's office in person," Mr. Fix said.

Passepartout thanked the man and left. Fix hurried to the consul's office.

"Consul," he said, "I hope you will *not* stamp

Mr. Fogg's passport."

"Why not?" the consul asked curiously. "If the passport is genuine, I cannot refuse."

"But I must keep this man here until I get an arrest warrant from London."

"Ah, that's a problem—for *you*," the consul said. "But I cannot—"

Just then Mr. Fogg entered the office. He told the consul that his next stop would be in Bombay, India.

"In that case, sir, a visa is not necessary," the consul explained.

"I know, sir," Phileas Fogg replied. "But your visa will prove that I came by Suez."

"Very well," the consul said.

As he stamped Phileas Fogg's passport, Fix watched, helplessly.

After giving Passepartout some orders, Mr. Fogg returned to the ship. There, he took up his notebook, where he had written:

Left London October 2
Reached Paris, October 3
Reached Turin, Italy, October 4
Arrived at Brindisi, Italy, October 5
Sailed on the Mongolia *October 5*
Reached Suez, Egypt, October 9

Total: Six and one-half days

While his master remained on board, Passepartout started to walk toward town. Fix hurried to catch up with him.

"Well, my friend," Fix said. "Did you get the visa stamp you wanted?"

"Yes, thanks," Passepartout replied.

"And now you're doing some sightseeing?" Fix went on.

"No. I must buy some shoes and shirts," Passepartout explained. "We left so quickly we brought very few clothes with us."

"But where is your master going in such a hurry?" Fix inquired.

"Around the world," Passepartout said.

"Around the world?" Fix cried out.

"Yes," said Passepartout, "—in eighty days! He says it's on a bet. But between us, I don't believe a word of it. It doesn't make common sense. I'm sure he has some other plan."

"Ah, your master is a character, is he?" Fix said with a friendly wink. "Is he rich?"

"No doubt," Passepartout agreed. "He's carrying an enormous amount of money. And the bank notes are all brand-new."

Fix frowned. "Have you known your master

for a long time?" he asked.

"Why, no," said Passepartout. "I was employed as his servant the same day we left London. Now we're traveling so fast I seem to be in a dream! Is Bombay far from here? That is our next stop."

"It's a ten-day trip by sea," Fix responded.

Passepartout blinked. "And in what country is Bombay?" he asked.

"India," Fix answered.

"India!" Passepartout exclaimed. Then he told Fix about leaving his gaslight on, but Fix wasn't listening. Instead, he was forming a plan. He would ask the London police to send an arrest warrant to Bombay. Then he would sail on the *Mongolia*, along with Phileas Fogg. Once Fogg set foot on English ground—in India—Fix would arrest him.

| 3 |

A Delay in Bombay

Time passed quickly on the *Mongolia*. As long as the sea was calm, the tables were crowded at breakfast, lunch, dinner, and supper. Between meals, passengers enjoyed games, music, and dancing.

But the Red Sea can be very wild at times. When the wind came up, the ship rolled fearfully. The passengers stayed below then. The pianos were silent, and the singing and dancing stopped.

What was Phileas Fogg doing all this time? Was he afraid the rough weather would delay his trip? If he worried, he showed no sign of it. He had four hearty meals a day—no matter how much the ship rolled. And he played game after game of whist.

As for Passepartout, he was pleased to discover a familiar face on board. It was

Mr. Fix! After the men exchanged names, Passepartout said, "I'm charmed to see you again, sir. May I ask where you are going?"

"Like you, to Bombay," Fix answered.

"How wonderful!" Passepartout cried out. "Have you made this trip before?"

"Several times," Fix said. "I work for the Peninsula Company, you see."

"Ah! Then you know India quite well?" Passepartout asked.

"Why—yes," Fix said. "A curious place. I hope you will have time to see the sights."

"Oh, I hope so, too, Monsieur Fix," said Passepartout. "I hope all this running around will end at Bombay. My master is in such a *rush*! A man should not spend his life jumping from a ship to a train and a train to a ship. Imagine pretending to go around the world in eighty days!"

"Perhaps this pretended trip hides a secret errand," Fix suggested slyly. "Perhaps your master is working for the government."

Passepartout shrugged. "I assure you I know nothing about it, sir," he confided. "But I'd give anything to find out."

The *Mongolia* reached Aden two days later.

As usual, Fogg and Passepartout went on shore to have their passports stamped. While Fogg returned to the ship, Passepartout wandered around the city. He was filled with wonder at the sights.

Very curious, very curious, he said to himself. *Travel is a wonderful thing if a man is eager to see something new!*

The *Mongolia* was due in Bombay on October 22. She arrived on the 20th. Phileas Fogg had gained two days. Calmly, he entered this fact in his notebook.

After docking at precisely 4:00 P.M., Mr. Fogg went straight to the passport office. As for the wonders of Bombay, he cared nothing. He ignored the famous city hall, its splendid library, its bazaars, and the fine pagoda on Malebar Hill. Instead, he went to a dining club. One of the dishes served to him was said to be "rabbit."

Mr. Fogg tasted it, but found it far from tasty. He rang for the landlord. When the man came, Fogg fixed his clear eyes upon him.

"Is this *rabbit*, sir?" Fogg inquired.

"Yes, my lord!" said the landlord. "Rabbit from the jungle."

Fogg frowned. "And did this rabbit meow

when it was killed?" he asked.

The landlord gasped. "*Meow*, my lord? What, a rabbit meow? I swear to you—"

"Please do not swear," Fogg insisted. "But remember this: Cats were once sacred animals in India. That was a good time."

"A good time for the cats, my lord?" the landlord asked.

"Good for the cats, and for travelers, also!" Fogg thundered.

While Mr. Fogg was at dinner, Mr. Fix went to the Bombay police office. He asked if the warrant from London had arrived. Unfortunately, it had not. Fix hoped very much that Fogg would stay in Bombay.

But Passepartout knew they would not be staying. Mr. Fogg had told him they were taking the 8:00 train to Calcutta. Now he wondered if the wager his master had mentioned was the true reason for their journey.

After buying the usual number of shirts and shoes, Passepartout wandered the streets of Bombay. It happened to be the day of a religious festival. Girls in rose-colored cloth danced by, light as air. Passepartout watched in awe, his mouth hanging open.

He wandered farther and came to the splendid pagoda on Malebar Hill. Curious, he stepped inside. He didn't know it was forbidden for Christians to enter this holy place. Even those who were allowed inside were required to leave their shoes at the door.

Passepartout was admiring the fine decorations when he suddenly was thrown on the floor! Then three furious priests tore off his shoes and began to beat him. But Passepartout was strong and agile. He quickly sprang upright and knocked down two of the priests with his fists and feet. Then he rushed out of the pagoda as fast as he could. He soon lost the third priest in a crowd.

Had he missed the train? At 7:55 P.M., a shoeless Passepartout arrived at the station, breathing hard. Phileas Fogg was waiting. So was Fix, who had followed Mr. Fogg to the station. He listened as Passepartout poured out his story to his master.

The man admits to entering the sacred pagoda, Fix said to himself. *This is a serious crime indeed. Now I've got them for sure!*

Fix took the train, too. No matter what, he would follow his quarry to Calcutta.

On the train, Fogg recognized one of his whist

partners from the *Mongolia*. The fellow's name was Sir Francis Cromarty.

Sir Francis's home was India. He knew a great deal about the country. But Phileas Fogg wasn't interested in stories about India. Instead, he told his own. Sir Francis wondered about the man. Did a human heart really beat beneath his cold exterior? To Sir Francis, Fogg's race to win a bet seemed foolish. *When Fogg died,* Sir Francis wondered, *would his life have done any good to himself or anyone else?*

Passepartout, however, was fascinated by India. The wandering ways of his youth came back to him. And he was now quite sure that his master was serious about his plan. So, he, too, began to worry about a delay.

Two days later, it happened. The train had stopped at a village called Kholby. The conductor explained that part of the cross-country railway had not yet been built.

Furious, Sir Francis thundered, "But we bought tickets all the way to Calcutta!"

"Yes," the conductor said. "But everyone knows there's a fifty-mile gap in the railway here. The next station is at Allahabad."

Sir Francis turned to Mr. Fogg. "This will

make you late," he warned.

"Oh, no," said Fogg. "It was foreseen."

"What!" said Sir Francis. "You knew—?"

"Not at all," Fogg replied. "But I knew a problem would come up sooner or later. I am already two days ahead of time. We shall reach Calcutta by October 25."

Passengers who'd known about the gap in the railway had hired all the available wagons, carriages, and ponies. Fogg and Sir Francis searched the village from end to end. They found nothing.

It was Passepartout who discovered the elephant. The animal's owner did not wish to rent him—even though Fogg offered 40 pounds an hour. Finally, Mr. Fogg bought the elephant for 2,000 pounds. After hiring a guide, they rode off through the forest.

It was a jolting ride, but Passepartout enjoyed it. He laughed as he bounced along like a clown on a springboard. That first day, they covered 25 miles.

But the next day, the elephant stopped just as they were entering a thick forest. Hearing voices and music coming their way, the guide hid the elephant in the trees.

The sounds came closer. Peering through

the trees, they saw a crowd. First came some priests, in long lace robes. Then came men, women, and children, singing a mournful song. Following behind was a young woman wearing gems and jewels from her head to her toes. She was followed by guards, armed with sabers and pistols. Some of them carried a corpse—the body of an old man, a rajah. His turban was decorated with pearls. His robe was made of the finest silk and gold.

Sir Francis turned his sad face to the guide. "It's a suttee," he whispered.

Nodding, the guide put a finger to his lips.

As the group disappeared into the woods, Fogg asked, "What is a *suttee*?"

"A human sacrifice," said Sir Francis. "The young woman will be burned, along with her husband's body."

"Burned *alive*!" Passepartout gasped. "Oh, the scoundrels!"

Fogg stayed perfectly calm. "Haven't the English been able to put a stop to such customs?" he asked.

"These sacrifices do not take place in most of India," Sir Francis explained. "But we have no power in certain territories."

"Where are they taking her?" Fogg asked.

"To a temple a mile or so from here," the guide said. "She will spend the night there. At dawn, the sacrifice will take place."

The guide led the elephant out of the trees.

"Wait!" Fogg said as he turned to Sir Francis. "Suppose we save this woman?"

Sir Francis looked shocked. "*Save* this woman, Mr. Fogg!" he exclaimed.

"I have twelve hours to spare," Fogg said.

Sir Francis was impressed. "Why, you are a man of heart, after all!" he cried out.

"Sometimes," Fogg quietly admitted. "But only when I have the time."

| 4 |

An Unexpected
Traveling Companion

Trying to save the young woman would be extremely risky. But Phileas Fogg didn't hesitate, and Sir Francis vowed to join him.

Passepartout was charmed by his master's idea. In spite of Fogg's icy exterior, the man must have a heart and soul!

But whose part would the guide take—the Indians or the rescuers?

After thinking it over, the guide said, "I will help you. But if we're taken, we will surely face horrible tortures—even death."

"That is foreseen," Mr. Fogg said. "I think we must wait until night before acting."

Agreeing, the guide told them what he knew about the young woman. She was a great beauty named Aouda. The daughter of a wealthy merchant, she'd received an English education in Bombay. Then she was left an orphan and—against her will—she was married to the old rajah. Now, his relatives believed that she should die by his side.

After traveling two miles, they stopped to wait behind a clump of trees. The pagoda was 500 feet away.

As the guide led the men through the trees, they passed a great stack of wood. On top of the stack was the rajah's corpse. The pagoda was now just 100 steps ahead.

"Come," the guide whispered.

The men slipped silently through the brush toward the rear of the temple.

They had only pocketknives for tools. But luckily, the pagoda was made of brick and wood. When one brick was removed, the rest would come easily.

They quietly set to work, but suddenly a cry was heard from inside the pagoda. They stopped. Had someone heard them?

They hurried back into the trees. Now guards appeared at the rear of the pagoda. They began to march back and forth.

Their plan had failed! Sir Francis shook his fists. Passepartout was beside himself. The guide gnashed his teeth. Fogg was quiet.

"Now there's *nothing* we can do!" Sir Francis hissed impatiently.

"There's still time," Fogg whispered. "Let us wait. We may have a chance later on."

Sir Francis stared at Fogg. What was he planning? Did he intend to grab the woman as she was about to be sacrificed? He couldn't believe that Fogg would be such a fool. Yet he agreed to wait.

An idea suddenly struck Passepartout. *It's crazy,* he said to himself. Then he thought, *Why not, after all?* Without saying a word, he slipped away from the others.

The hours passed. It was almost daylight. The sleeping Indians woke, and tambourines played. Cries and songs rose up as the doors of the pagoda swung open. Sir Francis's heart throbbed. He grasped Fogg's hand and realized that the man was holding a knife!

They watched as the young woman was led toward the stacked wood.

Fogg and the others followed the crowd. They saw the woman being laid out beside her husband's body. Then a torch was brought forward. The wood, soaked with oil, caught fire.

As Fogg started to rush forward, Sir Francis and the guide caught hold of him. Fogg pushed them aside. Then, suddenly, a cry of terror rang out. The Indians threw themselves to the ground.

The rajah was not dead! The "corpse" rose up quickly, took his wife in his arms, and stepped down from the wood pile. Clouds of smoke made him look like a ghost.

Men and women, guards and priests, lay with their faces down. They dared not look.

The rajah hurried toward Fogg and Sir Francis. They gasped. It was not the rajah, but Passepartout! He'd slipped through the smoke and delivered the young woman from death.

Fogg and the others ran into the woods and quickly boarded the elephant. They heard loud cries as they left the scene. A bullet whizzed through Fogg's hat! Their trick had already been discovered.

But the elephant was moving rapidly now. They were soon beyond the reach of the Indians' bullets and arrows.

Passepartout laughed gaily at his success. He'd already been a gymnast and a firefighter.

And now he had been a rajah!

The guide explained that Aouda was still in danger. Even if she went to another part of India, she'd be found out, and killed.

Phileas Fogg considered the matter as the guide led the elephant through the forest. At 10:00 A.M., they finally reached the train station at Allahabad. From there, they could continue on to Calcutta.

Aouda was still in a stupor from the fumes. Fogg took her to the waiting room in the station. He sent Passepartout out to buy a dress, furs, and other items for her to wear.

As the train was about to start, Fogg paid the guide for his help. Then he said, "Would you like to keep the elephant? He is yours."

"Sir, you have given me a fortune!" cried the guide. His eyes glistened with gratitude.

Before reaching Benares, the train's first stop, Aouda recovered from her ordeal. She was a lovely woman. Ebony hair framed her delicate white cheeks. Her body seemed to have been molded with a godlike hand. Imagine her surprise to wake up on a train—accompanied by three strangers!

Sir Francis explained how she had been saved.

She thanked her rescuers with tears, which said far more than words.

Knowing she could not stay in India, Aouda mentioned a cousin who lived in Hong Kong. Phileas Fogg offered to take her there, where she would be safe.

At Benares, Sir Francis said goodbye and went to join his troops. Passepartout and Aouda gave him a warm embrace of farewell. Fogg lightly pressed his hand.

At the station in Calcutta, a policeman was waiting for them.

"You must appear before Judge Obadiah," the officer said before leading them away.

In a few minutes, Fogg, Aouda, and Passepartout were standing in a courtroom.

"We're prisoners!" Passepartout exclaimed. "And the ship for Hong Kong leaves at noon!"

"Calm yourself. We shall be on board by noon," Fogg said quietly.

| 5 |

Leaving Passepartout Behind

Judge Obadiah, a round, fat man, entered the courtroom. "What crime are we accused of?" Fogg asked him.

At just that moment, the door opened, and three priests walked in.

"You are accused of entering a sacred place," Judge Obadiah said. "These three priests are witnesses. And here is the proof."

He placed a pair of shoes on his desk.

"My shoes!" Passepartout cried out. He'd forgotten all about his visit to the pagoda at Malebar Hill.

Passepartout did not notice Mr. Fix sitting in the corner. The detective had waited for Fogg's arrest warrant to arrive in Calcutta. When it didn't arrive, he'd sent for the priests who'd attacked Passepartout in the pagoda.

Poor Passepartout! He'd already foolishly admitted that the shoes belonged to him.

The judge sentenced Passepartout to 15 days in prison and a fine of 300 pounds. As Passepartout's master, Fogg was made to share the blame. He was sentenced to a week in prison and a fine of 150 pounds.

Fix rubbed his hands in satisfaction. Now Fogg would be in Calcutta an extra week! That should be more than enough time for the warrant to arrive.

"I will pay the bail," Fogg said, as he took a roll of bank notes from his bag.

"The money will be returned to you when your term has been served," the judge declared. "Meanwhile, you are free to go."

Fix followed them as they took a carriage to the harbor. He watched them board the *Rangoon*, a ship bound for Hong Kong. He stamped his feet in disappointment.

The rascal is off, after all! Fix muttered to himself. *And he let go of all that money! I'll follow him to the ends of the earth if I have to. But at the rate he's going, all of the stolen money will soon be spent.*

Fogg *had* spent a great deal of money. He'd bought tickets, clothes, an elephant, and more. Since leaving England, in fact, he had spent more than 5,000 pounds.

Mr. Fix left orders that the warrant should be sent along to Hong Kong. Then he, too, boarded the *Rangoon.*

Passepartout was surprised to see Fix on board the ship.

"Why, here you are, on the way to Hong Kong!" he said. "Are you going around the world, too?"

"No, no," Fix replied. "I shall stay at Hong Kong—at least for a few days."

Passepartout began to wonder if Fix was a spy for the Reform Club. He said to himself, *Imagine spying on Mr. Fogg—such an honorable man!* But he decided to say nothing to Mr. Fogg about his suspicions.

Mr. Fogg visited Aouda every day. She didn't know what to make of him. He was always very polite to her—but rather cold. When she looked at him, her eyes were as clear as the sacred lakes of the Himalayas. But it seemed that Mr. Fogg was not about to throw himself into this lake.

Near the end of the voyage, a storm blew up. The strong winds knocked the *Rangoon* about with fury and slowed their journey. At this rate, the captain said, they would reach Hong Kong 20 hours late.

Aouda was amazed at Fogg's calmness. It was as if he had foreseen the storm. But Passepartout was enraged at the weather. Everything had gone so well until now!

They arrived in Hong Kong 24 hours late. Passepartout was certain that they'd missed the ship for Yokohama, Japan.

But luck was with them. The ship, named the *Carnatic*, was still in port. One of her boilers was being repaired. She would not leave until the following morning—16 hours from now.

Fogg searched Hong Kong for Aouda's cousin. Unfortunately, he discovered that the man had gone to Europe two years ago. So Fogg invited Aouda to join their trip.

"But I cannot intrude—" she protested.

"You do not intrude," Fogg insisted. "Passepartout! Reserve three rooms on the *Carnatic* for Yokohama."

Passepartout was delighted. As he hurried off to buy tickets, he was not surprised to see

Mr. Fix again.

By now the detective was desperate. The warrant hadn't come! He was determined to keep Phileas Fogg in Hong Kong.

"Well, Mr. Fix," Passepartout said. "Hello again. Will you be coming with us to Japan and then on to America?"

"Yes," Fix hissed between his teeth.

"Good!" Passepartout exclaimed. "I knew you could not bring yourself to part from us. Let us go and reserve our rooms."

They were told that the ship's repairs were almost finished. She would be leaving that night, instead of the next morning.

Fix decided to make a bold move. He invited Passepartout to join him at a tavern. There, he ordered two bottles of wine. After Passepartout had drunk a fair amount, Fix told him that he was a police detective.

"Mr. Fogg's bet is a lie," Fix explained. "On September 28, fifty-five thousand pounds was stolen from the Bank of England. The description of the robber matches your master's age and appearance exactly."

"*Nonsense!*" Passepartout cried out. "My master is the most honorable of men!"

"How can you tell?" Fix asked. "You know almost nothing about him. The day you were hired, he decided to leave London. And he took a large amount of new bank notes with him! You must help me keep him here in Hong Kong. If you do, I'll share the two thousand-pound reward with you."

"Never!" Passepartout objected. "I won't believe Mr. Fogg is the robber. I've seen nothing but generosity and goodness in him! I would never betray him!"

"So you refuse?" Fix asked. "Very well. Then forget all I've said. Let us drink."

They did. Passepartout felt the effects of the wine. Before long he fell off his chair and slipped under the table.

At last! Fix thought. *Now Fogg won't know the* Carnatic *sails tonight. And if he does find out, he'll leave without this cursed Passepartout!*

If Mr. Fogg could ever be surprised, he might well have been that evening. For Passepartout failed to appear. The next morning he was still missing. So Fogg and Aouda took their luggage to the harbor. They hoped to find Passepartout there. But the servant was nowhere to be seen.

And neither was the *Carnatic*—which had sailed the night before.

Mr. Fix was waiting. "Were you hoping to sail on the *Carnatic*?" he asked.

"Yes, sir," Aouda declared.

"So was I, madam," said Fix. "But I have just learned that it has sailed without us."

Mr. Fogg didn't even blink. "There are other boats beside the *Carnatic*," he said calmly.

He offered his arm to Aouda and began to walk down the dock. As if attached to Fogg by an invisible thread, Fix followed.

After a short search, Mr. Fogg found a pilot boat, small and fast. Her master was John Bunsby. When Fogg said he wanted to go to Yokohama, the man hesitated.

Finally, he said, "I'm afraid I couldn't risk my little boat on so long a trip. But I could take you as far as Shanghai."

"You don't understand," Fogg explained. "I must catch the ship for San Francisco at Yokohama, not Shanghai."

"I do understand," Bunsby said, "but the trip to Yokohama starts from Shanghai."

Fogg offered him 100 pounds per day. In addition—if Bunsby reached Yokohama on time—he would have an extra 200 pounds.

Mr. Bunsby accepted. Then Fogg turned to Fix and invited him to go with them.

Fix was amazed. "Thank you, sir," he said. Fogg's kindness had made him feel very uncomfortable.

Before they left, Fogg and Aouda gave the police a description of Passepartout. And Fogg also left money to be spent in search of his missing servant.

Finally, it was time to depart. As the pilot boat left the dock, poor Passepartout was still lying on the tavern floor.

| 6 |

An Adventure in Yokohama

It was now early November—a risky time to cross the China seas. The water was very rough. Fogg, however, stood on the boat as steadily as a seasoned sailor. Aouda watched the white sails, which seemed to carry them along like the wings of a bird.

Fix had offered to pay for his share of the trip, but Fogg had refused. So he ate and drank at Fogg's expense. But he was still uneasy. Nevertheless, he was determined to follow the man until he could arrest him. *At least*, he thought, *Passepartout wasn't there to tell his master about Fix's true identity.*

Fogg was also thinking of Passepartout. He thought it was possible that his servant had boarded the *Carnatic*. Aouda agreed.

Meanwhile, the boat was making good progress. Bunsby was hopeful they would reach Shanghai in time. Then, one morning, the wind began to blow very hard.

Bunsby was worried. "I'm afraid a typhoon is coming up," he said to Fogg.

Rain hit the boat like bullets. The boat flew forward like a feather in the wind. Mountains of water rose on every side, but the crew managed her well.

They went through a terrible night. The boat shook and rolled violently. Aouda was exhausted but did not complain.

The next day brought calm. At noon they were 45 miles from Shanghai. The wind became calmer—and even calmer yet! The boat slowed down. As 6:00, they were still 12 miles from Shanghai.

Bunsby swore. Now it looked like he would lose his 200-pound reward!

Just then, an American ship appeared in the distance. It, too, was headed for Yokohama.

Fogg turned to Bunsby. "Signal her," he said quietly. "And hoist your flag."

Bunsby put the flag at half-mast—the signal

for help. Then the crew quickly loaded a small brass cannon on the forward deck.

"Fire!" Mr. Fogg cried out. A deafening boom of cannon fire filled the air.

* * * *

Where was Passepartout in the meantime? Three hours after Fix had left him in the tavern, he'd staggered to the *Carnatic*. Several sailors had carried him into a cabin.

A day later, Passepartout woke. He hurried to find his master so he could apologize. But Fogg and Aouda were not on board!

Now he saw Fix's trick. He'd deliberately been kept from meeting Fogg and Aouda. As a result, the *Carnatic* had sailed without them. Now Fogg's bet was lost! At this awful thought, Passepartout tore his hair. His own foolishness had cost his master everything!

Soon Passepartout would be arriving in Yokohama. What should he do when he got there? He hadn't a penny in his pocket.

When the *Carnatic* docked at Yokohama, Passepartout wandered the streets. He grew hungrier and hungrier. Finally, he traded some of his clothes for a hearty breakfast.

After eating, he headed toward the docks. It could be that a ship needed a cook or servant. Perhaps he might even work his way to San Francisco.

Then something caught his eye. A clown was carrying a sign through the streets. It read:

JAPANESE ACROBATS!
THE LONG NOSES WILL GIVE THEIR
LAST PERFORMANCE BEFORE LEAVING
FOR THE UNITED STATES

The United States! Passepartout thought. *That's just what I want!* He followed the clown to a theater. There, he asked for the man in charge. This was Mr. Batulcar.

"What do you want?" Batulcar asked.

"Would you be needing a servant, sir?" Passepartout asked politely.

"A servant!" cried Mr. Batulcar. "I have no use for a servant. Can you sing?"

"Yes, indeed," Passepartout answered.

"And you are a pretty strong fellow, eh?" Batulcar asked.

"Oh, yes," Passepartout said with a small smile, "especially after a good meal."

"But can you sing while standing on your head—with a top spinning on your left foot?

47

And with a sword balanced on your right foot?" Batulcar demanded.

"I—uh—I think so," Passepartout said.

It was settled. The performance was at 3:00 that afternoon. Passepartout was to be part of the human pyramid.

The performance began promptly. One performer wrote words with the smoke of his pipe. Another juggled lighted candles. The acrobats did amazing tricks on ladders, barrels, and balls.

Then it was time for the Long Noses. These performers wore noses made of bamboo attached to their faces. These noses were five, six—up to ten feet long! The Long Noses lay on their backs, while acrobats jumped from the tip of one nose to another.

The last act was the human pyramid. The first group of Long Noses lay on their backs. A second group climbed on top of their noses. Then a third group, and a fourth. As the pyramid slowly rose to the roof, the audience applauded loudly. Then suddenly, the whole pyramid fell like a house of cards! The fault was Passepartout's. He'd leapt from his place and dashed off into the audience—for he'd seen Phileas Fogg there!

"My master! My master!" he called out.

"You—*here*?" Fogg said coolly.

"I am!" Passepartout cried out.

"Very well, let us go to the ship, young man!" Fogg said.

Fogg, Aouda, and Passepartout hurried through the theater lobby. They were stopped by Batulcar, who was furious. But Phileas Fogg quickly soothed his feelings with a handful of pound notes.

* * * *

Fogg and Aouda had arrived in Yokohama on the 14th of November. When they found that Passepartout had been on board the *Carnatic,* Aouda was delighted. Fogg may have been delighted, too, but, as usual, he'd showed no sign of it.

Chance, or perhaps a second sense, had led Mr. Fogg to the theater. At first, he hadn't recognized Passepartout behind his strange nose. But the servant, while lying on his back, had immediately recognized his master.

The three travelers were now on board a ship called the *General Grant.* In 21 days, she was due to reach San Francisco. Luckily, the waters of the Pacific were quite calm. And Phileas Fogg, of course, was just as calm and quiet as the ocean.

Aouda had become quite enthusiastic about Fogg's journey. Now, any hint of delay made her impatient. In truth, she felt more than gratitude toward Fogg. But he seemed not to notice. Seeing this, Aouda kept her feelings to herself.

And where had Fix been all this time? In Yokohama, he'd finally received the warrant for Fogg's arrest. But, unfortunately for Fix, Fogg was no longer on English ground. The warrant was useless in Japan!

Well, thought Fix, *the rascal will return to England eventually. I'll stay with him—even across the Atlantic.* So he'd also bought a ticket to sail on the *General Grant.*

The next day, Fix was on deck when Passepartout saw him. Without a word, the angry servant grabbed Fix's neck and pounded him with his fists. That made Passepartout feel better—but Fix was rather rumpled.

"Please listen to me," Fix sputtered. "As long as Fogg was on English ground, I admit I tried to stop him. But now, my game has changed. I want Fogg back in England as quickly as possible—so I'll help him all I can."

Passepartout studied the detective's face. He

believed him.

"All right, then," Passepartout agreed.

"Are we friends?" Fix asked hopefully.

"Friends? No!" Passepartout snorted. "We are allies, perhaps. But at the smallest sign of treason, I'll twist your neck again!"

Fix understood.

On the third of December, the *General Grant* arrived in San Francisco. Fogg had neither gained nor lost a single day.

| 7 |

A Cross-Country Train Ride

It was 7:00 A.M. when Fogg, Aouda, and Passepartout stepped out on the dock in San Francisco. Since the next train to New York would leave at 6:00 P.M., they took a carriage to wait at the International Hotel.

After breakfast, Fogg left with Aouda to have his passport stamped. Passepartout had heard stories of Indians attacking trains, so he went to buy some revolvers. Fogg didn't think guns would be necessary, but he'd told Passepartout to do as he thought best.

Just outside the hotel, Fogg came upon Mr. Fix. The detective acted as if he were quite surprised to see him. He said he hoped to keep Mr. Fogg company on his return trip to England.

Fogg graciously said that it would be his honor. Then he invited Fix to join them on their walk.

They soon found themselves on a busy thoroughfare called Montgomery Street. A great crowd had gathered there. Some people shouted, "Hurrah for Camerfield!" Others cried, "Hurrah for Mandiboy!" It was a political rally.

"Perhaps we should get out of the way," Fix said. "There may be danger."

Fogg shook his head and they walked to the end of the street. This part of the crowd was even more excited. Fists were thrown. Boots and shoes were flying through the air. Then the crack of revolvers rang out.

Fix was alarmed. "Let's go now!" he cried out. He wanted to be sure that Fogg returned to London in one piece.

Suddenly a hubbub broke out behind them. Another crowd was rushing toward the first group. Mr. Fogg, Aouda, and Fix were caught between them! The two men were knocked around as they tried to protect Aouda. When a big fellow with a red beard tried to hit Fogg, Fix rushed between them and took the blow himself.

Fogg gave the big fellow a withering look.

"*Yankee!*" he hissed scornfully.

"*Englishman!*" the fellow growled. "We will meet again!"

"Whenever you please," Fogg said coldly.

"What is your name?" the man demanded.

"Phileas Fogg. And yours?"

"Colonel Stamp Proctor."

The crowd swept by. Fix's face was bruised, but he wasn't seriously hurt.

"I will come back to America to find this Colonel Proctor," Fogg said calmly. "It's wrong to treat an Englishman this way!"

At 6:00, they got on board the train. It was to be a 3,786-mile trip. Fogg expected to reach New York in seven days.

As the passengers slept, the train sped through California. Early the next morning, it had reached Nevada. The passengers looked out on vast prairies and distant mountains.

About noon, the train stopped. A huge herd of buffalo was blocking the track. The travelers watched and waited as thousands of buffalo streamed across the track.

Passepartout was furious at the delay. He longed to empty his revolvers at the beasts. "What a country!" he grumbled.

It was three hours before the last buffalo finally

crossed the track. Then the train went on and reached Utah that night. Next came Wyoming.

At a town called Green River, Aouda saw several passengers get on board. One of them was Colonel Stamp Proctor! She waited until Mr. Fogg was asleep. Then she told Mr. Fix and Passepartout that Proctor was aboard.

"It would be terrible," she said, "if Mr. Fogg should meet Colonel Proctor. He must *not* see him under any circumstances!"

Passepartout agreed. "If possible, we must keep my master in this car," he said.

It was the detective who found a way to do this. When Mr. Fogg awoke, Fix suggested a game of whist. Happy to return to his favorite pastime, Fogg sent Passepartout out to buy cards. Soon the game began.

Now we've got him, Passepartout thought to himself. *He won't budge.*

The train had just crossed the Rocky Mountains when the card game was interrupted by a violent whistle—which stopped abruptly, along with the train.

Fogg sent Passepartout to investigate. He discovered a red blockade across the track. Some 30 or 40 passengers, including Colonel Proctor, were already standing outside. They were talking excitedly with the conductor and the engineer. Colonel Proctor's voice was one of the loudest.

The problem was that the bridge up ahead appeared to be unsafe. The engineer was worried that the weight of the train might make it collapse.

"We'll have to walk to Medicine Bow, the next town," the conductor said. "Another train will meet us there in six hours."

"Six *hours!*" Passepartout wailed.

"Yes," the conductor said. "And it will take us nearly that long to reach Medicine Bow."

"But Medicine Bow is only a mile from here," one of the passengers pointed out.

"That's so. But it's on the other side of the creek," the conductor said patiently.

"Why can't we cross the creek on a boat?" Colonel Proctor demanded.

"That's quite impossible," the conductor replied. "The creek is swollen with rain. It is a rapid. We'll have to walk 10 miles before it's narrow enough to cross."

Colonel Proctor swore long and loudly. Passepartout was beside himself. Even Mr. Fogg's money was useless in this situation.

Just then the engineer finally spoke up. "Gentlemen," he said, "perhaps there *is* a way to get over after all."

"On the bridge?" a passenger asked.

"On the bridge," the engineer declared.

"With our train?" the passenger asked.

"Yes, with our train," said the engineer. "By moving at the very highest speed, we'd have a good chance of making it across."

Several passengers nodded. They thought this was an excellent idea.

"To me, that plan seems—uh—unwisely dangerous," Passepartout said.

He had another idea. He suggested that it would be safer for the passengers to cross the bridge on foot. Then the empty train—made much lighter—could cross over on its own.

Unfortunately, no one listened to his idea. Fully loaded with passengers, the train backed up for almost a mile. Then, it began to move forward, faster, and faster. Finally, it was speeding ahead at nearly 100 miles an hour.

As quick as a flash, the train passed over! The engineer, however, couldn't slow it down. It raced five miles beyond the station before it finally stopped. No one knew that the bridge collapsed just after the train had crossed over.

| 8 |

Captured by the Sioux

Now the train chugged steadily forward across the great plains. In only four days, it was due in New York.

Mr. Fogg and his partners continued their game of whist. Fogg was playing well, and luck was with him. He was about to make a bold move by playing a spade.

Suddenly, an insolent voice snarled, "Ha! I think I'd play a diamond if I were you."

The players looked up. It was Colonel Proctor! Aouda's face turned pale.

Fix jumped up and said, "I know you, sir. You are the man who insulted me. I insist that you deal with me now."

"Pardon me, Mr. Fix," Fogg interrupted. "But I believe that this is *my* affair."

"I'm ready, Fogg," the colonel thundered.

"Just name the place and the weapons."

Fogg hesitated. "Sir, I'm in a great hurry to return to England," he said. "Will you agree to a duel six months from now?"

"It's now or never," Proctor insisted. "We'll fight at the next stop—Plum Creek."

"Very well," Fogg said coolly.

But the train didn't stop at Plum Creek. "We're twenty minutes late," the conductor explained. "I'm sorry, gentlemen. But why don't you fight as we go along?"

Both Fogg and Colonel Proctor nodded.

The conductor led them to an empty car. Mr. Fogg stood at one end and the colonel at the other. Each man carried two revolvers. At the sound of the train whistle, they agreed to begin shooting.

Suddenly, wild cries and crackling gunfire filled the air. Fogg and Proctor looked out the window in amazement. A band of Sioux Indians was attacking the train!

A few Indians had jumped onto the engine and knocked out the engineer. As he fell, his body had pushed the throttle full forward. Now the train was plunging forward at a truly dangerous rate.

Most of the passengers carried revolvers.

They tried to fight back as the Indians entered the train cars. Aouda was courageous from the start. She leaned out a broken window and shot at the Indians.

The next station was Fort Kearny, just two miles away. There were plenty of soldiers at the fort. But someone had to stop the train, and the engineer was out cold. Who could bring the engine to a halt?

The conductor, fighting alongside Mr. Fogg, was shot down. "Do something!" he cried out as he fell. "Unless this train is stopped in five minutes, we're lost!"

"It shall be stopped," Phileas Fogg said confidently. He was just rising from his seat when Passepartout spoke up.

"Stay, master! I have an idea."

Passepartout opened the door of the car and sneaked outside. Then he slipped under the train. Holding onto the chains under the train, he crept along from car to car. In this endeavor, his skills as a former acrobat were serving him very well!

At last, he reached the engine and loosened the safety chains. After a sharp jolt, the engine was freed from its cars. Now it sped off, leaving the cars behind. They continued to roll ahead,

but finally stopped—just 100 feet from the Fort Kearny station.

Soldiers hurried up to the train, their rifles at the ready. In the face of this unexpected force, the Sioux ran off.

Many passengers had been wounded, but none were killed. Colonel Proctor had fought bravely but was seriously injured. Aouda was safe, and Fogg hadn't been touched. Fix's arm was slightly wounded. But three travelers had been taken prisoner by the Sioux—and one of them was Passepartout! Aouda was frantic.

Fogg knew that the loss of a single day would ruin his plans. But he didn't hesitate.

"Never fear, I will find him, living or dead," he declared.

"Ah, Mr. Fogg!" Aouda cried. She clasped his hands and covered them with tears.

At Fort Kearny, Fogg asked if soldiers would be sent to rescue the prisoners.

"Why should I risk fifty men just to save three?" the captain asked.

"Very well," Fogg said coldly. "I'll go alone."

The captain was impressed. "You are a brave man," he said. "Very well, you shall not go alone." He turned to his soldiers. "I need thirty volunteers!" he called out.

Every soldier raised his hand. The captain had only to choose his men.

Fix stepped forward. "May I go with you, Mr. Fogg?" he asked hopefully.

"You will do me a favor if you stay with Aouda," Fogg replied. "If something should happen to me—"

Fix turned pale. He didn't dare lose track of Fogg. Should he let him go off by himself? He stared at the stubborn Englishman—and had to lower his eyes. Fogg's face was so calm, so frank, he could not refuse him.

"All right, I will stay," he said.

As they took off after the Sioux, Fogg offered the soldiers a reward of $5,000 if they saved the prisoners.

It was then a little before noon.

Fix and Aouda waited in silence. Aouda thought about Fogg's courage. Fix wondered if he'd been a fool for letting Fogg get away.

Around 2:00 P.M., the lights of the missing engine appeared. While the engineer was unconscious, it had traveled 20 miles past the station! When he came to, he'd stopped the train immediately. Then he'd run it in reverse until it reached the Fort Kearny station.

The passengers cheered. Eager to continue their journey, they hurried to board the train. The conductor warned Aouda that they were leaving right away.

"But the prisoners—" she sputtered.

"I cannot delay the trip," said the conductor. "We're already three hours late. If you wish to come, please get on board."

"I will not go," Aouda said.

As the hours passed, the weather turned cold. Aouda walked outside and stared into the distance. She watched and listened. There was nothing to see, nothing to hear.

When night fell, a snowstorm blew in. Aouda was still waiting and praying. Her heart was filled with fear and sadness.

Nothing happened until 7:00 the next morning. Then shots rang out in the distance. The rescuers were returning!

Fogg was marching at the head of the group. Passepartout followed behind him, along with the soldiers and the other two travelers—weary from fighting the Sioux.

All were welcomed with joyful cries. As promised, Fogg rewarded the soldiers with $5,000. Aouda took Fogg's hand and held it tightly. She was too moved to speak.

Meanwhile, Passepartout looked around for the train. "Where is it?" he cried.

"Gone," said Fix. But he had a suggestion. A man named Mudge could transport them on a kind of sled. Mudge had spoken to him about it the night before.

Fogg went to look at the sled. It had runners like an ordinary sled, but it also had a mast and sails. Mudge said that if the wind was good, they could reach Omaha, Nebraska, in five hours.

There, they could catch a train to Chicago.

They climbed onto the sled. What a journey! The travelers huddled together, too cold to speak. High winds swept the odd-looking vehicle across the snowy plains at 40 miles an hour!

After several hours, Mudge saw familiar landmarks. He drew in the sails, and the sled slowed to a stop. Mudge pointed to the town ahead. They'd reached Omaha.

Fogg gave Mudge a generous reward when they arrived at the train station. Then they quickly boarded a waiting train.

On December 10, they reached Chicago. Late on the 11th, they reached New York. But the steamship bound for Liverpool, England, had left only 45 minutes earlier!

| 9 |

Commandeering
the *Henrietta*

The ship for Liverpool seemed to have been Fogg's last hope. All the other steamers were bound for other ports.

Passepartout was crushed. He felt it was his fault. Instead of helping his master, he'd put obstacles in his path! But there was not a word of blame from Fogg.

They took a carriage from the station to a hotel, where they passed the night. Everyone but Fogg slept poorly.

The next day, Fogg went alone to the docks. He found a trading ship, the *Henrietta*, that was leaving in an hour.

The captain, Andrew Speedy, told Fogg that he never took passengers. "They're too much in the way," he said. Also, he was headed for France, not England.

But Fogg persisted. "France will do nicely, as well. Will you take me there?" he asked.

Speedy shook his head. "Not even if you paid me 200 dollars," he said.

"Ah! But I'm offering 2,000," Fogg said.

"Apiece? For four of you?" Speedy gasped.

"Apiece," Fogg assured him.

Speedy quickly decided that passengers might not be such a bother after all.

An hour later, they left New York.

The next day, a lone man stood on the *Henrietta*'s deck. He was clearly in command of the ship. One might think this was Captain Speedy. But, no, it was Phileas Fogg, esquire. Captain Speedy was locked up in his cabin, crying out furiously.

What had happened was simple. Mr. Fogg had bribed the crew to take him to Liverpool, England. The greedy sailors were quite happy to accept the man's money and follow his orders. Fogg immediately took charge.

Passepartout was delighted. He formed warm friendships with the sailors and amazed them with his acrobatic feats. His good humor seemed to spread to everyone.

As to Fix, he had no idea how Fogg had pulled it off. He was completely confused.

On December 13, in the middle of a terrible storm, they passed the coast of Newfoundland. Somehow Fogg kept the *Henrietta* straight on course, without even slowing down. Great waves sometimes broke over the deck—but the ship passed on safely.

On the 16th of December, the engineer was worried. "You should know that we had only enough coal to get to Bordeaux," he said to Mr. Fogg. "But Liverpool is farther. Unless we slow down, we'll run out of fuel."

"Feed the fires until the coal runs out," Fogg replied. Then he sent Passepartout to fetch Captain Speedy. Poor Passepartout had been asked to unchain a tiger!

"Where are we?" Captain Speedy demanded as he was led out on deck. His face was purple with rage.

"We're 770 miles from Liverpool," Fogg answered calmly.

"*Pirate!*" Captain Speedy screamed.

"I would like to buy your ship, sir," Fogg said calmly.

"No! By all the devils, *no*!" Captain Speedy howled in protest.

"Then I shall have to burn her—at least the upper part. The coal is giving out, you see," Fogg explained coolly.

"Burn my ship?" Speedy shrieked. "Burn a ship worth fifty thousand dollars!"

Fogg handed the man a roll of bills. "Here is sixty thousand," he said.

Speedy forgot his anger in an instant. The *Henrietta* was 20 years old. Sixty thousand was a fabulous price.

Fix nearly had a fit as he watched the money change hands. All told, Fogg had so far spent almost 20,000 pounds!

The *Henrietta* now belonged to Phileas Fogg. First he had the cabins burned, then the bunks and the spare deck. Next came the masts, the rafts, and the railings. Finally, the ship was nothing but an iron hulk. Yet even so, they were running out of fuel.

On the 20th of December they saw the coast of Ireland. Fogg knew what to do. He had only 24 hours to reach London.

In Dublin, the capital, they immediately boarded a ship that was bound for Liverpool.

It was 11:40 A.M. on December 21 when they stepped onto the dock. Fogg was only six hours away from London.

Now on English ground, Fix presented Fogg with the arrest warrant. "You, sir, are really Phileas Fogg?" he asked.

"I am," Fogg said with a cool smile.

"I arrest you in the Queen's name!" the detective cried out triumphantly.

Passepartout tried to attack Fix, but two policemen held him back. Aouda was thunderstruck as Fogg was led away.

In his prison cell, Fogg put his watch on the table and watched the hands move. Aouda and Passepartout waited outside. They could not leave. Passepartout was desperate. If only he'd told his master who Fix really was!

When the clock struck one, it occurred to Fogg that his watch was two hours fast.

Two hours! On an express train, he could reach London at a quarter to nine! Fogg's forehead wrinkled ever so slightly.

At 33 minutes past two, he heard sounds outside. Doors were being opened down the hall. Then Fogg could hear Passepartout and Fix talking. His eyes brightened.

The door of his cell swung open. There stood Passepartout, Aouda, and Fix.

Fix hurried toward Fogg. He was out of breath. "Sir—" he stammered. "Sir—forgive me. The robber looked *exactly* like you. He was arrested three days ago. You—are free!"

Phileas Fogg was free! He walked up to Fix and knocked him down with one blow.

"Well done!" Passepartout exclaimed.

A few minutes later, Fogg, Aouda, and Passepartout were in a cab headed for the train station. But again they were too late. The express train had already left.

They had just five and a half hours to get to London. But what could they do? They took the next train, which was much slower. And there were many delays.

When Fogg finally stepped off the train in London, it was ten minutes before nine. Oh, no! Having made a tour of the world, he was five minutes late. He'd lost the wager!

| **10** |

Winning More than Money

Phileas Fogg quietly returned to his home. He still had 20 thousand pounds in the bank. But he owed it all to the gentlemen at the Reform Club. Even if he'd won the bet, he wouldn't have made money. He'd spent too much. His bold bet had totally ruined him.

Passepartout had hurried to his room when they arrived home. There, he turned off the gas, which had been burning for 80 days. Then he sat down and waited. He was afraid of what his master might do.

Aouda was also very anxious. "The poor man must not be left alone for an instant!" she told Passepartout.

For once, Fogg did not go to the Reform

Club. Instead, he shut himself in his room. Like a faithful dog, Passepartout sadly waited outside the door.

Then, at 7:30 P.M., Fogg left his room and went to find Aouda.

"Madame," he said, "will you forgive me for bringing you to England? When I brought you away from India, I was rich. I counted on putting aside some of my fortune for you. But now I am ruined."

Aouda took his hand. "And will you forgive *me* for delaying your trip?" she asked. "I have contributed to your ruin."

"Madame, you could *not* remain in India," Fogg reminded her. "At any rate, I beg you to accept what little money I have left."

Aouda's heart was breaking. "And what will become of you, Mr. Fogg?" she asked.

"I have need of nothing," Fogg replied.

"But you should not face the future alone. Your friends—" she began.

"I have no friends," Fogg interrupted.

"Your relatives—" Aouda went on.

"I no longer have any relatives," said Fogg.

Aouda rose and took his hand. "Solitude is a sad thing, Mr. Fogg," she said. "If you like, you may have a wife and a friend from this moment on. Will you have me for your wife?"

Mr. Fogg rose from his chair. His eyes shone and his lips trembled. He felt the sincerity and sweetness of this noble woman.

"I love you," he said simply. "And I am entirely yours!"

"Ah!" cried Aouda. She closed her eyes and pressed his hand to her heart.

Fogg called for Passepartout. When he saw his master holding Aouda's hand, he understood immediately. His round face began to glow as brightly as the tropical sun.

Fogg told Passepartout to find Reverend Wilson. He wanted the marriage to take place tomorrow.

"Tomorrow—Monday?"

"Yes, Monday."

Passepartout happily hurried off. It was five minutes past eight.

* * * *

It is time now to tell what had happened in England *before* Fogg arrived.

On December 17, the real bank robber, James Strand, was arrested. Until then, most people had thought Phileas Fogg was a criminal. After

Strand's arrest, Fogg was again regarded as an honorable gentleman.

The newspapers were running stories about the bet again. And just as before, Phileas Fogg "bonds" were being traded.

The five friends at the Reform Club were in suspense. Would Fogg return to England in time? Telegrams were sent to America and Asia for news of his journey. But there was no news at all. And the police had no idea what had become of Mr. Fix.

By Saturday evening, all of London was in suspense. A crowd gathered near the Reform Club. Inside, the five friends waited.

At 20 minutes to eight, the engineer, Stuart, cleared his throat loudly. "Gentlemen, Phileas Fogg has only 20 minutes left," he announced.

"What time did the last train arrive from Liverpool?" asked Flanagan, the brewer.

"At exactly twenty minutes past seven," said Ralph, the bank director.

"Very well, gentlemen," Stuart continued smugly, "if Fogg had been on that train, he'd be here by now. I think our bet has been won."

"I agree," Flanagan added. "Mr. Fogg's project was foolish to begin with, of course. There were certain to be delays on the trip."

Sullivan, another banker, spoke out. "And we've had no word of him."

At this moment, it was 20 minutes to nine.

"Just five minutes more," Stuart said.

The men looked at each other. They were all very anxious, but trying not to show it. Fallentin suggested a game of cards.

Now it was 18 minutes to nine.

The players took up their cards, but they could not keep their eyes off the clock. The minutes had never seemed so long!

Occasionally, the silence was broken by the murmur of the crowd outside.

"It's sixteen minutes to nine," Sullivan said.

One minute more, and they would win the bet! As if by agreement, they stopped their game and counted the seconds.

At the 55th second, a loud cry was heard in the street. People were *cheering*.

The players rose from their seats.

At the 57th second, the door of the room swung open. Phileas Fogg appeared, followed by an excited crowd. In his calm voice, he said, "Here I am, gentlemen."

Indeed, it was Phileas Fogg in person.

The reader will kindly remember that Passepartout had been sent to see Reverend Wilson. This was to arrange for a marriage ceremony the following day. He'd left the Reverend Wilson's house at 35 minutes past eight. What a state he was in as he ran home! His hair was wild, his hat was missing, and he could hardly speak.

"Master!" gasped Passepartout. "Marriage — impossible—tomorrow—is *Sunday*!"

"No, Monday," Mr. Fogg corrected him.

"No, sir. Today—is Saturday!"

"Impossible!" Fogg snorted.

"*Not* impossible!" Passepartout cried out. "You've made a mistake of one day! We arrived twenty-four hours ahead of time. Now we have only ten minutes left!"

Phileas Fogg hurriedly jumped into a cab. He promised the driver 100 pounds if he made it to the Reform Club on time.

At exactly a quarter to nine, his friends were there waiting for him.

Phileas Fogg had traveled around the world in 80 days!

He'd won his bet!

The reader will also remember that Phileas

Fogg was an extremely exact gentleman. How did he make this error of an entire day? He'd simply forgotten that he'd gained one day by traveling eastward. If he'd been traveling westward, he would have lost a day.

Fogg had won 20,000 pounds. But having spent 19,000 pounds of his own money on the trip, he had gained only one thousand pounds. His object, however, had not been to gain money, but to *win*. So he decided to divide the one thousand pounds between Passepartout and the unlucky detective. As a true gentleman, he held no grudge against Mr. Fix.

Fogg was, however, still a gentleman of very precise habits. So he deducted the gas bill from Passepartout's share.

That evening, Fogg turned to Aouda. "Is our marriage still agreeable to you?"

"Ah, Mr. Fogg!" Aouda exclaimed. "I should ask *you* that question. You thought you were ruined, but instead you are still rich."

"Pardon me, madam," Fogg interrupted. "My fortune belongs to you. If you had not suggested marriage, my servant would not have gone to Reverend Wilson's. I would never have known I'd made an error, and—"

"Dear Mr. Fogg!" Aouda cried out.

"Dear Aouda!" Fogg sighed in return.

* * * *

The marriage took place the next day. Glowing with joy, Passepartout gave the bride away. Had he not saved her? And did he not deserve this honor?

Phileas Fogg had traveled around the world in 80 days. To do this, he'd used ships, carriages, boats, trains, a strange sled, and an elephant. The whole time, he had remained exact and cool-headed. But what was his greatest gain from this long and weary journey?

Why, nothing less than a charming woman who made him the happiest of men. Wouldn't you travel around the world for less?

Activities

Around the World in Eighty Days

BOOK SEQUENCE

First, complete the sentences with words from the box. Then, number the events to show which happened first, second, and so on.

hours	house	Calcutta	pagoda	discovery tour
Bombay	seconds	*Henrietta*	rajah	*General Grant*
Chicago	*Carnatic*	reconsider	San Francisco	

____ 1. The _____ sails without Fogg, Aouda, and Fix.

____ 2. The _____ carries the travelers to San Francisco.

____ 3. Fogg wins his bet by a margin of three _____.

____ 4. Fogg bets that he can _____ the world in 80 days.

____ 5. While visiting the _____, Passepartout is attacked.

____ 6. In Omaha, the travelers board a train for _____.

____ 7. Many Englishmen _____ Fogg's hasty departure.

____ 8. As the *suttee* ceremony begins, Passepartout pretends to be the _____.

____ 9. Fogg pays Captain Speedy a fortune for the _____.

____ 10. Fogg and Passepartout head for _____ when the leave Egypt.

____ 11. In _____, Fogg and Fix accidently get embroiled in a political rally.

____ 12. Passepartout explores Fogg's _____ from top to bottom.

____ 13. Passepartout makes an amazing _____ when he visits Reverend Wilson.

RECALLING DETAILS
Reread Chapter 1 and answer below.

1. About how many years ago does this story take place?
   a. 75 years
   b. 130 years
   c. 100 years

2. In French, what does *passepartout* mean?
   a. "jack-of-all-trades"
   b. "trusted servant"
   c. "go everywhere"

3. Why did Phileas Fogg avoid most people's company?
   a. He didn't want to waste time.
   b. He was a very shy man.
   c. He was leading a secret life.

4. How much had been stolen from the Bank of England?
   a. 55,000 dollars
   b. 55,000 pounds
   c. 55,000 gold coins

5. What words did the newspapers use to describe the thief?
   a. "smooth talking"
   b. "very handsome"
   c. "well-dressed"

SENTENCE COMPLETION

Reread Chapter 3 and complete the sentences with words from the box.

pagoda	conductor	gained	captain	dangerous
sacrifice	train	rabbit	burned	ceremonies
rajah	errand	curious	transportation	

1. Fogg and Sir Francis search for _____ to Allahabad.

2. Cromarty explains that a *suttee* is a human _____.

3. Reaching Bombay, Fogg calculates that he has _____ two days.

4. Fix suggests that Fogg's trip hides a secret _____.

5. The _____ explains that there's a 50-mile gap in the railway.

6. Passpartout visits a splendid _____ on Malebar Hill.

INFERENCE
Reread Chapter 4 and answer below.

1. Why did Fogg wonder if the guide might side with the Indians instead of the rescuers?

   _____

   _____

   _____

2. Why did Fogg suggest waiting until night before going after Aouda?

   _____

   _____

   _____

3. Why did Fogg think it would be wise to take Aouda to Hong Kong?

   _____

   _____

   _____

4. Something happened that made Sir Francis "shake his fists" and the guide "gnash his teeth." What had happened?

   _____

   _____

   _____

CHARACTER STUDY

A. Reread Chapter 6 and circle two words that describe each character's attitudes and actions.

1. **Phileas Fogg**
   cowardly   generous   bold   despicable

2. **Mr. Fix**
   forthright   secretive   determined   lazy

3. **Passepartout**
   acrobatic   pathetic   mystified   apologetic

4. **Aouda**
   grateful   enthusiastic   aggressive   spiteful

B. Write a character's name next to his or her line of dialogue.

1. _____ "Hoist your flag!"

2. _____ "I admit I tried to stop him."

3. _____ "We are allies, perhaps."

4. _____ "Would you be needing a servant, sir?"

5. _____ "Let us go to the ship, young man."

FINAL EXAM

A. Circle the letter to correctly answer each question or complete each statement.

1. How much did Fogg bet that he could make a tour of the world in 80 days?
   a. 20,000 dollars
   b. 20,000 pounds

2. How could Fogg's emotional makeup best be described?
   a. composed, unperturbed, remote
   b. forlorn, withdrawn, melancholy

3. What did Passepartout contribute to the success of Fogg's journey?
   a. absolute confidentiality
   b. several daring deeds

4. Fogg said he didn't belive in the unforeseen. But one completely *unforeseen* outcome of his journey was
   a. losing a day
   b. regaining his reputation

B. Answer each question in your own words. Write in complete sentences.

1. Where did Fogg get the idea that a person could travel around the world in 80 days?

   _____

   _____

   _____

2. Why was Fix confident that he'd recognize Fogg when he got off the ship in Egypt?

   _____

   _____

   _____

Answers to Activities
Around the World in Eighty Days

BOOK SEQUENCE
1. 7/*Carnatic* 2. 8/*General Grant* 3. 13/seconds 4. 2/tour
5. 5/pagoda 6. 10/Chicago 7. 3/reconsider 8. 6/rajah
9. 11/*Henrietta* 10. 4/Bombay 11. 9/San Francisco
12. 1/house 13. 12/discovery

RECALLING DETAILS
1. b   2. c   3. a   4. b   5. c

SENTENCE COMPLETION
1. transportation 2. sacrifice 3. gained 4. errand 5.
conductor 6. pagoda

CHARACTER STUDY
A. 1. generous, bold   2. secretive, determined
    3. acrobatic, apologetic   4. grateful, enthusiastic
B. 1. Fogg   2. Mr. Fix   3. Passepartout
    4. Passepartout 5. Fogg

FINAL EXAM
A. 1. b 2. a 3. b 4. a 5. b
B. 1. He read it in a newspaper article.
    2. He said that he had a sixth sense about such things.